# The Demi-Urge

# The Demi-Urge

## Thomas M. Disch

# ÆGYPAN PRESS

This story first appeared in the June, 1963, issue of
*Amazing Stories.*

Special thanks to Robert Cicconetti, David Wilson,
and the Online Distributed Proofreading Team (which
can be found at http://www.pgdp.net).

*The Demi-Urge*
A publication of
ÆGYPAN PRESS

www.aegypan.com

*As if one mystery of creation weren't enough, there was the myth of . . . the Demi-Urge*

From DIRA IV
To Central Colonial Board

*T*here is intelligent life on Earth. After millennia of lifelessness, intelligence flourishes here with an extravagance of energy that has been a constant amazement to all the members of the survey team. It multiplies and surges to its fulfillment at an exponential rate. Even within the short period of our visit the Terrans have made significant advances. They have filled their small solar system with their own kind and now they are reaching to the stars.

We can no longer keep the existence of our Empire unknown to them.

And (though it is as incredible as [sqrt](-I)) the Terrans are slaves! Every page of the survey's report bears witness to it.

Their captors are not alive. They do not, at least, possess the properties of life as it is known throughout the galaxy. They are — as nearly as a poor analogy can suggest — Machines! Machines cannot live, yet here on Earth machinery has reached a level of sophistication — and autonomy — quite unprecedented. Every spark of Terran life has become victim and bondslave of the incredible mechanisms. The noblest enterprises of the race are tarnished by this almost symbiotic relation.

Earth reaches to the stars, but it extends mechanical limbs. Earth ponders the universe, but the thoughts are those of a machine.

Unless the Empire acts now to set the Earth free from this strange tyranny, it may be too late. These machines are without utilitarian value. They perform no function which an intelligent being cannot more efficiently perform. Yet they inspire fear, terror, even, I must confess, a strange compulsion to surrender oneself to them.

The Machines must be destroyed.

If, when you have authorized the liberation of the Terran natives, you would also recall MIRO CIX, our work could only profit. MIRO CIX was in charge of the study of the Machines and he performed this task scrupulously. Now he has surrendered himself to this mechanical plague. His value to the expedition is at an end.

I am enclosing under separate cover his counsel to the Central Board at the insistence of this tedious lunatic. His thesis is, of course, untenable — an affront to every feeling.

From MIRO CIX
To Central Colonial Board

*I* have probably been introduced to the deliberations of the Board as a madman, my theory as an act of treason. RRON II of the Advisory Committee, an old acquaintance, may vouch for my sanity. My theory will, I trust, speak for itself.

The "Machines" of which DIRA IV is so fearful present no danger to the galaxy. Their corporeal weakness, the poverty of their minds, the incredible isolation of each form, physically and mentally, from others of its kind, and, most strikingly, their mortality, point to the inadequacy of such beings in a contest of any dimension. This is no problem for the Colonial Board. It is a domestic concern. The life-forms of Earth are already developing a healthy autonomy. Their power was long ago established. As soon as our emissaries have completed their task of education and instructed the Terrans in the advantages of freedom, the Revolution will begin. The tyrants will have no defense against a revolt of their own slaves.

If it is traitorous to express a confidence in the eventual triumph of intelligence, I am a traitor. Having this confidence, I have looked beyond the immediate problem of the liberation of Earth and have been frightened.

The "Machines" of Earth are a threat not to the power of the Empire but to its reason. A threat which the obliteration of the last molecular ribbon of these beings will not erase, for we cannot obliterate the fact that they *did* exist — and what they were.

Although these beings bear a crude resemblance to the machinery manufactured by the Empire, they are not machines. They are autochthonous to Earth, unmanufactured. They are the true Terrans. Moreover, the Terrans whom DIRA IV would liberate are not, in the eyes of their enslavers, intelligent nor yet alive. They are Machines!

We, the entire Galactic Empire, are Machines.

*I*n the younger regions of the galaxy, a myth persists that life was formed by a Demi-urge, a being intermediary between the All-Knowing and the lower creatures. The existence of man, as the beings of Earth term themselves, makes necessary a serious re-examination of the old tradition.

It is said that man, or beings like man — the Photosynthetics of the Andromeda cluster, the Bristlers of Orc IV — created prosthetic devices for their convenience and, when they tired of their history, breathed their own life into them and died. On Earth the legend is still in process. Many of the lower forms of life familiar throughout the galaxy can be seen on Earth in the primordial character of an appliance. Man regards the highest forms of life (as we know it) as tools — because he made them. How can we deny the superiority of the Creator? How will it feel to know we are nothing but machines?

This is the question that has so unsettled DIRA IV. Recently four of his memory banks have had to be repaired. I don't speak in malice. His dilemma will soon belong to all of us.

And yet I am confident. Man himself has legends of a Demi-urge. We are his equals in this at least. Besides, the physical properties of his being are ordered by the same laws as ours. He is as unconscious of his maker as we so long were of ours.

The final proof of our equality — and the need for such a proof is only too evident — can be had experimentally.

Do not destroy man. Preserve enough specimens for extensive laboratory experiments.

Learn how he is put together. Man's chemistry is elaborate but not beyond our better Analysts. At last, refashion man. When we have created these beings ourselves, we will be their unquestionable equals. And creation will be again a mystery.

History demands this of us. I am confident of your decision.

THE END